A Note for Teachers, Parents and Other Adults

These are the things whose fruits we eat in this ~~life~~ but whose full reward awaits us in the Wo~~rld to~~ Come:

Honoring parents, acts of kindness, arriving early at the house of study morning and evening, hospitality to strangers, visiting the sick, helping the needy bride … devotion to prayer, and bringing peace between people—but the study of Torah is equal to them all.

—from the Babylonian Talmud, Tractate Shabbat 127a

It's a … It's a … It's a Mitzvah is inspired by this Talmud teaching and aims to focus young kids on a contemporary introduction to these good deeds and to God's commandments—*mitzvot.* By highlighting the age-appropriate good deeds mentioned in the Talmud verse and others, it broadens the use of the word *mitzvah* beyond "sacred commandment" to reflect the way most people use it today to include *g'milut hasidim*—acts of lovingkindness. *Mitzvot* include many acts of kindness but they also include other, equally important, holy deeds like learning from the Torah, attending a seder, and resting and playing on Shabbat.

This lively book is filled with likeable animal characters who, through their actions, perform good deeds and acts of lovingkindness of all types. Through playful vignettes, children engage with Jewish wisdom and how the sages instruct us to behave toward each other. For each good deed, the Mitzvah Meerkat congratulates and celebrates the animals' actions with the following exclamation, "It's a … it's a … it's a mitzvah!" The fun-sounding refrain is repeated to encourage children to join in with the reader. We explain each good deed in a sidebar. This gives you an opportunity to ask the child or group of children, "What is the good deed here?" and spark a conversation. Hopefully, the children will guess the act of kindness before you even read the sidebar.

We hope as children become familiar with this book, they will be inspired to become *menschen*—kind souls who think about and help others.

Enjoy!

— Liz Suneby and Diane Heiman

It's a ... It's a ... It's a Mitzvah

Library of Congress Cataloging-in-Publication Data
Heiman, Diane.
It's a— it's a— it's a mitzvah / Diane Heiman and Liz Suneby ; Illustrations by Laurel Molk.
p. cm.
Summary: This lively picture book for children ages 3-6 is filled with amiable animals, who through their actions demonstrate age-appropriate mitzvot, including welcoming new friends, forgiving mistakes, respecting elders, and sharing food with the hungry. It engages children through playful illustrations; likeable animal characters, including Mitzvah Meerkat, the narrator; humor and the repetition of the fun-to-say phrase "It's a ... it's a ...it's a mitzvah!" that encourages children to chime in as the words are repeated throughout the book. Side notes on each spread explain the specific mitzvah in every vignette. With this aside, parents and teachers have an opportunity to ask the child or group of children, "What is the good deed here?" and spark a conversation without preaching. Children will see how everyday kindness is the beginning of a Jewish journey and a lifetime commitment to *tikkun olam* (repairing the world)—Publisher.

ISBN 978-1-58023-509-9 (hc)

1. Commandments (Judaism)—Juvenile literature. I. Suneby, Elizabeth, 1958– II. Molk, Laurel. III. Title. IV. Title: It is a mitzvah. V. Title: It is a— it is a— it is a mitzvah.
BM520.7.H395 2012
296.1'8—dc23
2012003703

ISBN 978-1-68336-772-7 (pbk)

Jacket and interior design: Tim Holtz

Published by Jewish Lights Publishing
www.jewishlights.com

Award-Winning Children's Books from Jewish Lights

Adam & Eve's First Sunset
God's New Day
by Sandy Eisenberg Sasso
Illustrations by Joani Keller Rothenberg
Explores fear and hope, faith and gratitude, in a way that kids will understand.
For ages 4 & up. 9 x 12, 32 pp, Full-color illus.,
HC, 978-1-58023-177-0

Also available—a board book for kids 0–4:
Adam & Eve's New Day 978-1-59473-205-8
(SkyLight Paths)

Around the World in One Shabbat
Jewish People Celebrate the Sabbath Together
by Durga Yael Bernhard
Take your child on a colorful adventure to share the many ways Jewish people celebrate Shabbat around the world. *Shabbat Shalom!*
For ages 3–6. 11 x 8½, 32 pp, Full-color illus.,
HC, 978-1-58023-433-7

Because Nothing Looks Like God
by Lawrence Kushner and Karen Kushner
Illustrations by Dawn W. Majewski
Shows how God is with us every day, in every way.
For ages 4 & up. 11 x 8½, 32 pp, Full-color illus.,
HC, 978-1-58023-092-6
Also Available: Teacher's Guide by Karen Kushner:
For ages 5–8. 8½ x 11, 22 pp,
PB, 978-1-58023-140-4

But God Remembered
Stories of Women from Creation to the Promised Land
by Sandy Eisenberg Sasso
Illustrations by Bethanne Andersen
Four different stories of women briefly mentioned in biblical tradition and religious texts, but never explored.
For ages 8 & up. 9 x 12, 32 pp, Full-color illus.,
Quality PB, 978-1-58023-372-9

Cain & Abel
Finding the Fruits of Peace
by Sandy Eisenberg Sasso
Illustrations by Joani Keller Rothenberg
A beautiful recasting of the biblical tale. A spiritual conversation-starter about anger and how to deal with it, for parents and children to share.
Ages 5 & up. 9 x 12, 32 pp, Full-color illus.,
HC, 978-1-58023-123-7

The 11th Commandment
Wisdom from Our Children
by The Children of America
"If there were an Eleventh Commandment, what would it be?"
For all ages. 8 x 10, 48 pp, Full-color illus.,
HC, 978-1-879045-46-0

For Heaven's Sake
by Sandy Eisenberg Sasso
Illustrations by Kathryn Kunz Finney
Isaiah, a young boy, searches for heaven and learns that it is often found in the places where you least expect it.
For ages 4 & up. 9 x 12, 32 pp, Full-color illus.,
HC, 978-1-58023-054-4

God in Between
by Sandy Eisenberg Sasso
Illustrations by Sally Sweetland
If you wanted to find God, where would you look? Teaches that God can be found where we are.
For ages 4 & up. 9 x 12, 32 pp, Full-color illus.,
HC, 978-1-879045-86-6

God's Paintbrush
Special 10th Anniversary Edition
by Sandy Eisenberg Sasso
Illustrations by Annette Compton
Invites children of all faiths and backgrounds to encounter God openly through moments in their own lives—and help the adults who love them to be a part of that encounter.
For ages 4 & up. 11 x 8½, 32 pp, Full-color illus.,
HC, 978-1-58023-195-4

Also available—a board book version for kids 0–4:
I Am God's Paintbrush 978-1-59473-265-2
(SkyLight Paths)

God's Paintbrush Celebration Kit
A Spiritual Activity Kit for Teachers and Students of All Faiths, All Backgrounds
by Sandy Eisenberg Sasso & Rev. Donald Schmidt
Illustrations by Annette Compton
This indispensable, completely nonsectarian teaching tool is designed for all religious education settings.
Five sessions for eight children ages 5–8.
9 x 12, 40 Full-color activity sheets and teacher folder,
978-1-58023-050-6

Award-Winning Children's Books from Jewish Lights

God Said Amen
by Sandy Eisenberg Sasso
Illustrations by Avi Katz
A stubborn Prince and Princess show children and adults how self-centered actions affect the people around us, and how by working together we can work with God—to create a better world.
For ages 4 & up. 9 x 12, 32 pp, Full-color illus., HC, 978-1-58023-080-3

In God's Hands
by Lawrence Kushner and Gary Schmidt
Illustrations by Matthew J. Baek
Brings to life a traditional Jewish folktale, reminding parents and kids of all faiths and all backgrounds that each of us has the power to make the world a better place—working ordinary miracles with our everyday deeds.
For ages 5 & up. 9 x 12, 32 pp, Full-color illus., HC, 978-1-58023-224-1

In God's Name
by Sandy Eisenberg Sasso
Illustrations by Phoebe Stone
Poetic text and vibrant illustrations. Shares the ultimate harmony of belief in one God by people of all faiths, all backgrounds.
For ages 4 & up. 9 x 12, 32 pp, Full-color illus., HC, 978-1-879045-26-2

Also available—a board book version for kids 0–4:
What Is God's Name? 978-1-893361-10-2
(SkyLight Paths)

Also available in Spanish: El nombre de Dios
9 x 12, 32 pp, Full-color illus.,
HC, 978-1-893361-63-8 (SkyLight Paths)

In Our Image
God's First Creatures
by Nancy Sohn Swartz
Illustrations by Melanie Hall
A playful new twist to the Genesis story, God asks all of nature to offer gifts to humankind—with a promise that the humans would care for creation in return.
For ages 4 & up. 9 x 12, 32 pp, Full-color illus., HC, 978-1-879045-99-6

Also available—a board book version for ages 0–4:
How Did the Animals Help God?
978-1-59473-044-3 (SkyLight Paths)

The Kids' Fun Book of Jewish Time
by Emily Sper
A unique way to introduce children to the Jewish calendar—night and day, the seven-day week, Shabbat, the Hebrew months, seasons and dates. Interactive.
For ages 3–6. 9 x 7½, 24 pp, Full-color illus., HC, 978-1-58023-311-8

Noah's Wife
The Story of Naamah
by Sandy Eisenberg Sasso
Illustrations by Bethanne Andersen
A new story celebrating the wisdom of Naamah, whom God calls on to save each plant on earth in the Great Flood.
For ages 4 & up. 9 x 12, 32 pp, Full-color illus., HC, 978-1-58023-134-3

Also available—a board book version for ages 0–4:
Naamah, Noah's Wife 978-1-893361-56-0
(SkyLight Paths)

The Shema in the Mezuzah
Listening to Each Other
by Sandy Eisenberg Sasso
Illustrations by Joani Keller Rothenberg
In a divided world where the one who shouts the loudest often gets the most attention, a story about compromise and listening.
For ages 3–6. 9 x 12, 32 pp, Full-color illus., HC, 978-1-58023-506-8

What Makes Someone a Jew?
by Lauren Seidman
Using simple rhymes, language and photos children can relate to, this bright, friendly book helps preschoolers and young readers understand that you don't have to look a certain way to be Jewish.
For ages 3–6. 10 x 8½, 32 pp, Full-color photos, Quality PB, 978-1-58023-321-7

What You Will See Inside a Synagogue
by Rabbi Lawrence A. Hoffman
and Dr. Ron Wolfson
Photographs by Bill Aron
Foreword by Sandy Eisenberg Sasso
Colorful photographs set the scene for concise but informative descriptions of what is happening, the objects used, the clergy and laypeople who have specific roles, the spiritual intent of the believers and more.
For ages 6 & up. 8½ x 10½, 32 pp, Full-color photos, Quality PB, 978-1-59473-256-0

SkyLight Paths is a sister imprint of Jewish Lights.

It's a... It's a... It's a
MITZvah

For everyone who has ever touched
my life with acts of kindness, big or small. —LS

For Bruce, Allie, and Carolyn, because of you
I know that love is boundless. —DH

Grateful acknowledgment is given to Stuart M. Matlins, publisher of Jewish Lights, and
Emily Wichland, vice president of Editorial and Production, for having faith in our ideas
and enabling us to share them, and to Laurel Molk for giving spirit to our words.

It's a... It's a... It's a MiTZVah

Liz Suneby and Diane Heiman
Illustrations by Laurel Molk

JEWISH LIGHTS Publishing
www.jewishlights.com

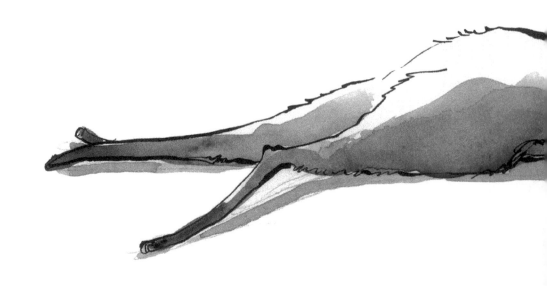

It's a ... it's a ...
it's a mitzvah!

It's a mitzvah
to share
food with
someone who
is hungry.

I'm hungry as a bear.

Here, take one sandwich ...

or two, or three, or four, or five, or six, or seven …

Whew, I'm getting tired. I guess I'm not a young buck anymore!

It's a ... it's a ... it's a mitzvah!

It's a mitzvah to help someone who is older.

Grandpa, would you like to rest under that tree? I'll wait with you.

It's a ... it's a ...
it's a mitzvah!

It's a mitzvah
to forgive
someone for
making a
mistake.

Whoops—one stick too many!
I broke our cozy new lodge.

No worries.
We will rebuild it.

Let's recycle the plastic bottles.

Good thinking, Joey! Please hop on over to the recycle bin for me.

It's a ... it's a ... it's a mitzvah!

It's a mitzvah to take care of the Earth.

It's a ... it's a ... it's a mitzvah!

It's a mitzvah to return something someone has lost.

Peter, I found your mitten!

It's a ... it's a ...
it's a mitzvah!

You are such a
good swimmer,
and I
barely made it
across the
shallow end.

It's a mitzvah
to cheer on
your friends.

You're doing really well;
you'll be a great swimmer
soon. I only wish I could
run half as fast as you.

It's a ... it's a ...
it's a mitzvah!

It's a mitzvah
to take care
of someone
who is sick.

Mr. Katz, we heard Lizzy is sick. Here's some homemade chicken soup with oodles of noodles to make her feel better.

Thank you.
Lizzy will love it.

It's a ... it's a ...
it's a mitzvah!

It's a mitzvah
to give
tzedakah
(charity).

It's so nice to knit for
those in need.

Hurry up. You're taking way too long.

There's no need to start a fight.
Give Zoe one more minute.
You can have my turn.

It's a ... it's a ...
it's a mitzvah!

It's a mitzvah
to help make
peace.

Hey, Ellie, it's Friday.
What should we do tonight?

Come to my
house and
share the
loving spirit
of Shabbat.

It's a ... it's a ...
it's a mitzvah!

It's a mitzvah to
enjoy Shabbat
with family and
friends.

It's a ... it's a ...
it's a mitzvah!

It's a mitzvah
to honor your
parents.

I love it when
you give us
bedtime
snuggles.

I love it when you
read us bedtime
stories and sing us
bedtime songs.

And I love you
all the time!

We know what a mitzvah is.

We know you can't touch it.

We know you can't smell it
(unless it's homemade
chicken soup).

We know you can't buy it.

We know a mitzvah by the warm feeling of happiness in our hearts when we do good deeds.

Mitzvah is a way of life.

That's a ... that's a ... that's a mitzvah!

www.ingramcontent.com/pod-product-compliance
Lightning Source LLC
Jackson TN
JSHW071956131224
75386JS00050B/1792